IZZY

The Cowgirl Corgi

Written and Illustrated by Kady Toole

Outskirts Press, Inc.
http://www.outskirtspress.com

Paperback ISBN: 978-1-9772-3846-7

Cover and Interior Illustrations © 2021 Kady Toole.

Outskirts Press and the "OP" logo are trademarks belonging to Outskirts Press, Inc.

PRINTED IN THE UNITED STATES OF AMERICA

Welcome to Saddle Summit...

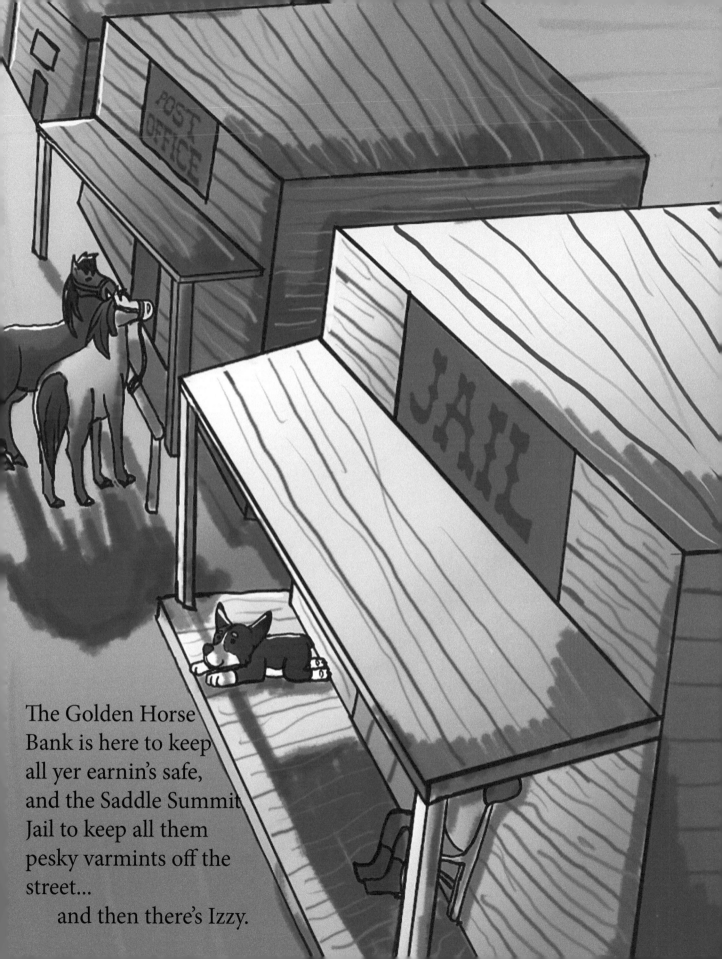

The Golden Horse Bank is here to keep all yer earnin's safe, and the Saddle Summit Jail to keep all them pesky varmints off the street...

and then there's Izzy.

Izzy is Sheriff Stone's dog, not that the sheriff notices her much. When he's not roundin' up bandits, the sheriff is always takin' care of his mustangs.

Feedin' em...

And cleanin' their toenails.

There ain't nothin' the sheriff wouldn't do fer them there horses.

The sheriff's mustangs were known all over the
territory for always bringin' in the bad guys.
Bandits far and wide feared the sound of
their highly manicured clip-clop.

The Bad Bunch
– Greedy Gus, Lanky Luke, and Jughead Jud –
robbed the Golden Horse Bank while the mustangs were
off getting their monthly pedicures.

They held up the bank, blew the safe door, and took off with all of Saddle Summit's hard-earned money. They loaded it up in a wagon and headed for the hills - free and clear!

Sheriff Stone was
beside himself. How would
he ever catch the Bad Bunch
without his clip-cloppin' horses?

Izzy knew what to do. She would stop the Bad Bunch herself. She grabbed her red bandana, and off she went.

She caught up to the Bad Bunch and
the wagon full of money at Filley Falls.
Izzy had a plan. She would use her corgi cuteness
to earn the Bad Bunch's trust… and that's just what she did.
She pat-patted right up to their campfire wearing her cutest
smile and wiggling her most adorable butt-nub wiggle.

pat pat....
   pat pat....
      pat pat....

As the Bad Bunch ate their dinner around the fire, Izzy snuck into the wagon and grabbed a bag of Saddle Summit's money. She pranced past Luke – wiggling her butt nub all the way.

Izzy stopped next to the falls, tauntin' the Bad Bunch with the bag of money. Luke took after Izzy like a steam engine as he reached to grab the bag. At the last second, Izzy bobbed to the left, and over the falls went Luke.

Seeing a branch sticking out over the falls, Izzy threw the money bag she was carrying, and it caught on the branch.

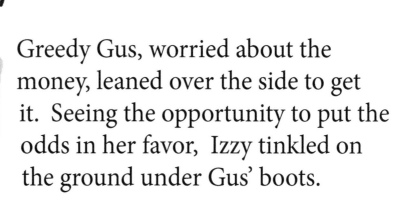

Greedy Gus, worried about the money, leaned over the side to get it. Seeing the opportunity to put the odds in her favor, Izzy tinkled on the ground under Gus' boots.

The dirt turned into mud and Gus slipped – right over the edge of the falls.

Jughead Jud, seeing Gus go over the edge, leaned out to help.

Izzy jumped up and gave Jud one quick "bop," and over the falls he went.

Izzy grabbed the money bag, threw it back on the wagon, doused the fire, grabbed the reins of the horses, and headed back to Saddle Summit.

Izzy handed the reins to the sheriff

and finally got the attention she had always wanted …

and more.

THE END.

CPSIA information can be obtained
at www.ICGtesting.com
Printed in the USA
BVHW021142040621
608820BV00009B/277